Published in a limited first edition
of 250 copies signed by the author and the artist.

This is copy 75

Other works of fiction by Robert Kelly

The Scorpions

Cities

The Cruise of the Pnyx

A Transparent Tree

Doctor of Silence

Cat Scratch Fever

Queen of Terrors

The Logic of the World

Robert Kelly

TEN
NEW
FAIRY
TALES

With drawings by
Emma Polyakov

McPherson & Company
Kingston, New York

2019

Text: Copyright © 2019 by Robert Kelly
Drawings: Copyright © 2019 by Emma Polyakov
All rights reserved.

McPherson & Company

P.O. Box 1126 Kingston, NY 12402

WWW.MCPHERSONCO.COM

1 3 5 7 9 10 8 6 4 2   2019 2020

Library of Congress Cataloging-in-Publication Data

Names: Kelly, Robert, 1935- author. | Polyakov, Emma O'Donnell, illustrator.
Title: Ten new fairy tales / Robert Kelly ; with drawings by Emma Polyakov.
Description: Limited, first edition. | Kingston, N.Y. : McPherson & Company,
  [2019] | Summary: A collection of fairy tales, written in the Christmas
  season of 2016, featuring spectral foxes, a telepathic ape and antelope, a
  lady snake with a black silken umbrella, and more.
Identifiers: LCCN 2019001049 | ISBN 9781620540374 (pbk. : alk. paper)
Subjects: | CYAC: Fairy tales.
Classification: LCC PZ8.K372 Ten 2019 | DDC [Fic]--dc23
LC record available at https://lccn.loc.gov/2019001049

Typeset in Mrs Eaves and Mr Darcy.
Design by Bruce McPherson.

PRINTED IN U.S.A.

for

Jane Madill
Ani Dechi

CONTENTS

The Fox and the Other Side
⋅⋅⦃9⦄⋅⋅
The Ape and the Antelope
⋅⋅⦃13⦄⋅⋅
The Boy in the Camel
⋅⋅⦃17⦄⋅⋅
The Umbrella
⋅⋅⦃21⦄⋅⋅
The Priest's Peculiar Wife
⋅⋅⦃29⦄⋅⋅
The Cat and the Butterfly
⋅⋅⦃37⦄⋅⋅
The Girl in the Curtains
⋅⋅⦃43⦄⋅⋅
Shadow Talk
⋅⋅⦃49⦄⋅⋅
The Leper's Touch
⋅⋅⦃55⦄⋅⋅
The Rainbow
⋅⋅⦃63⦄⋅⋅

The Fox and the Other Side

FOR several years there was a fox's den behind our summerhouse. A foxes' house I should say, because the den was home to a red fox at some times, a black fox at others. I had never seen a black fox.

I used to sit screened in, sprawled in a big old armchair, safe from the mosquitoes of eventide, insistent as church bells. I wanted to see the black fox close up, but never managed to do so. Only when I was far across the lawn would he appear, moving slow enough for me to see him clearly, but not too clear.

Anyhow, I liked the red fox better, it was a real foxy fox, color of marmalade, color of cream, with a sly gait and a furtive glance here and there—he knew how to be a fox, looking like a four-foot version of any high school student slouching home.

I read up on foxes and found that there

were black foxes, green foxes, and blue foxes as well as the ordinary kind they called 'rufous' though red would do well enough. "These are," I read in the big nature book, "the foxes of the other side. Watch out for them. When they appear they sometimes seize the territory of the rufous or common fox. There are known instances, furthermore, where the apparition of a black fox has heralded, or perhaps even induced, changes in the visual apparatus of human spectators, so that ever after one color seems suddenly much (as one patient described it) 'louder than before, louder than it ought to be.' Such examples of chromatic peril are not uncommon in the tropics, but rare in North America."

The next time I saw the black fox I closed my eyes right away, and called out to him,

Why do you change our eyes? To my surprise, he answered lucidly, in an accent that reminded me of a friend of my wife from Slovenia: I change you to make you see the other side — that's where I come from and where you are going. Get ready.

After silence, I opened my eyes. No fox. I walked over to the summerhouse, over grass that seemed preposterously green.

The Ape and the Antelope

ONCE upon a time there lived an ape and an antelope. The time is actually now, and they live in different countries but they know how to talk to each other, using a scientific principle awaiting detection: sciosophy, they call it, the wisdom of shadows. Seems that if you dance around and make shadows of a certain sort and in a certain order, the air picks the shadows up as signals which can be decoded anywhere on the planet by those in the know. The ape (in Namibia) and the antelope (in Wyoming) were two such cognoscenti, who'd gotten to know and trust each other (what harm could one do to other?) some years before during a partial eclipse of the moon, partial in Africa, total in the West. They had much to talk about, each describing at length the customs and obstacles of their region.

One day the antelope had a run-in with some hunters, thickish white men in colorful warm coats. She liked the colors but was afraid. When they began shooting at her, she ran away and hid in a little ravine, where she urgently shadowed a message to her friend the ape.

"When they're white, run away," the ape explained.

"I did that, I'm hiding now, what should I do?"

"Well, you can run fast but bullets run faster, I can't run much myself, so try to outsmart them. Try this: repeat the following formula while striking the earth with your, let's see, right forefoot: *Agamagus Hariganus Farnabayus Hilderskoot*. At the last syllable, toss your horns in the air — you do have horns, don't you?"

"They're small, I'm a girl."

"Well, any size will do. You know the formula?"

Animals are very good at remembering, since they don't have books to scatter their memories. So the antelope said Yes, but asked the ape to repeat it one more time. The ape did so, and the antelope mouthed the syllables to fix them in mouth.

Then she stood up and bellowed the phrase,
AGAMAGUS HARIGANUS
FARNABAYUS HILDERSKOOT
while she pounded the hard-packed winter earth.

An eighth of a mile away, one of the hunters got a sudden toothache, and recalled that he had accidentally skipped his scheduled visit to the dentist. And the other hunter, with equal suddenness, remembered an appointment in town, an important one, money was involved. So both hunters turned around and went home.

Antelope and ape shared their pleasure, the antelope promising to think of some way to be of help to the ape, the ape, embarrassed, saying no need for that. But it is fortunate, isn't it, that humans have such poor memories.

The Boy in the Camel

ONCE upon a time a boy was born inside a camel. No one knew why. As he grew, the boy learned to make his way around, first in the animal, then later, as the animal when it moved around in the world.

Sometimes the boy slipped his little legs into the big front legs of the camel, sometimes into the hind legs, and so learned to walk. If he had had language already, he would have said I walk twice. But as it was, he just walked.

And there was plenty of room in the hump for his head. So as he grew, he never felt squeezed in or uncomfortable. Though it is only honest to remark that he never liked the food the camel give him, though the water the animal gulped up was tasty, and helped him tolerate the bland food. He became after a while something of a connoisseur of water — springs, oases, lakes, rivers, standing pools, he knew them all.

His years passed pleasantly enough, travelling about, walking, trotting, or all curled up asleep under the hump, cradle-rocked by the camel's gentle lurching. The camel taught him Camelese (with a heavy Saharan accent) and the boy taught the camel a language he thought was Humanish that he had made up, so the two got on well together. The boy had no idea that there were other humans, or if there were, that some of them might live outside their camel. The camel, though, in chatting with his kin and kind, suspected that few other camels had boys living inside them. It made him feel very special indeed, but he was careful not to let on to the boy how unusual their situation was. And he never disclosed it to other camels either, or anybody else, until one fine day he came to the oasis called El Fna.

There he found a great wodge of freshly cut khat, a mild intoxicant leaf for humans that causes dimmed wits and sharpened dreams, people like dullness with pictures in it, so khat is popular. Strange to find so much of it just lying there. But so he did, and gobbled it all right up. Almost at once, the inside boy fell fast asleep and dreamed about stars and stones and bowls of milk. But the camel got very excited, danced around and started bellowing this and that, old camelish jokes and puns and bawdy songs. When he trotted up to a pond nearby and spread his legs to bend to drink, he saw his own form mirrored in the water, and cried out, O most beautiful travel camel, how sprint and springy thy leaping about, how graceful thy formy-warm, who would know a talking boy lives all inside?

Now as it happened a Djinn was passing overhead at the moment, and as usual paying no attention to the clamor drunk or sober of camels — until the last part of the camel's boast.

Hm, thought the Djinn, a talking boy. I could use one of those. And with deft, magic, long, many-jointed djinn-fingers he painlessly opened the camel's side, plucked out the still-sleeping boy, zipped up the camel, told the animal O you're better off this way, tucked the boy under his wing and flew away.

It didn't take the boy long to get used to his new life, but he never did get used to the bright daylight. Historians credit him with the invention of sunglasses. His gait was peculiar, even as a grown man, lurching, abruptly swooping down a little at the waist. He became a scholar and writer. famous in Arabic literature as Abd el-Batn, servant of the interior, master of esoteric lore.

Christmas Day 2016

The Umbrella

ONCE upon a time, and not so very long ago at that, a traveler was making his way west from Bengal, and was crossing the flat fields of Bihar, which was then and likely still is now, the poorest state in India. As he pedaled along, he reflected that for a country with a population of a billion India could manage at times to look deserted. Here, for instance, with jungly places on the left and rice fields to the right, the road straight and empty, our traveler hadn't seen a soul in half an hour of conscientious cycling.

All the more surprising to see, upright, open and unfurled, a gentleman's umbrella standing straight up out of the muddy paddy. This was no parasol or beach umbrella, this was a black silken affair such as a rich businessman in Kolkata would shield him-

self with on his way in drizzle from the bank to the club. An umbrella standing up in an empty field. A mystery. Our traveler was intrigued, and wheeled his bicycle off the road and along the muddy edge of the field. Fortunately, the umbrella was stuck only a few feet in from the edge, so the traveler left his machine standing up, its wheels wedged deep enough in the mud to remain vertical. Then, delicately, he picked his way off the edge into the quaggy places en route to the umbrella. He looked about carefully, anxious to avoid insects and snakes. He didn't like snakes.

But a snake is just what he found: a big black cobra wrapped around the bamboo handle of the umbrella. So that's why the umbrella was upright! The traveler stopped, stood still, very afraid. Then the cobra spoke; as you might expect, the snake spoke English. The traveler, who had benefitted from a good education among the nuns of Saint Josaphat's Academy in Shiliguri, could speak English fairly well.

"I hope you were not thinking of stealing

my umbrella — it happens to be from a very fancy outfitter in Holborn."

"No, O Serpent of good family, I came only to observe this wonder, an umbrella open in an empty field, no person nearby. Excuse my intrusion."

"Am I not a person?"

"I meant no human person, your lordship."

"Ladyship. I am a female of the species."

"I'm sorry again, my Lady."

"I am not your lady. I am my lady."

"How clumsy I am, please excuse me again, I meant no insult."

"I believe you. You speak fairly well for a man from Bengal. Can you say 'snake'?"

"Shnake."

"I thought so. You found it odd that a poor serpent should shield herself from the heat or the sun and the pelting of the rain?"

"No, no, your Lady. I didn't see you, only the umbrella."

"You must understand that those of us who live flat on the ground all the time must take pains to avoid intemperate aggressions from the upper air — excessive heat and light and water and (I have been told) even ice and snow in the mountains. An umbrella is simple prudence. And naturally it is unfurled — what benefit a closed canopy?"

"I understand, now I know why the umbrella is here I will take my leave with thanks for the explanations."

"But what is that thing stuck in the ground over there?" said the snake, gesturing towards the upright bicycle. You must understand that there's only one way a snake can gesture, by pointing his head (in this case her head) at the thing intended. Her gesture now, towards the cycle, terrified the traveler, supposing it to be the first movement of a catastrophe. Luckily, though, he got the drift of her movement, which anyhow had stopped with the mere repointing of her glance.

"That is a bicycle, your Lady, it is mine, I have ridden it all the way from the Valley of the Teesta, and am on my way to Bodh Gaya, to pay my respects to Lord Buddha, a notable incarnation of Vishnu, we have been taught."

"Never mind that. How does it move?"

"I pump the pedals with my feet, and that makes the wheels turn, and as they turn, the machine moves ahead."

"Do not use that f-word around us. It is a painful word, redolent of the immense sacrifices our kind have made for your sake, so that we live in perfect contact with the wise earth, and can slip in and out of earth with ease, bringing wisdom and jewels and healing substances. Here, for you."

So saying, the cobra spat out a glittering amethyst. It trickled over to the traveler.

"May I pick it up?" he asked with fear.

"Certainly, it is yours now. It will help you remember the earth you roll across, and those who live on and in it. Perhaps someday it will help you to learn what we know."

Timidly, our traveler bent, slowly picked up the amethyst, and bowed deeply to the snake.

"Thank you, your Lady!"

The snake closed her eyes, lowered her head. It seemed like an acknowledgement of what he had said, so the traveler backed away towards his machine, tugged it out of the mud, kicked the spokes clear, dragged it back to the road, hopped on and went swiftly away. He cycled for a few moments before he realized he wasn't quite sure about which direction he'd been headed before he saw the umbrella.

Boxing Day 2016

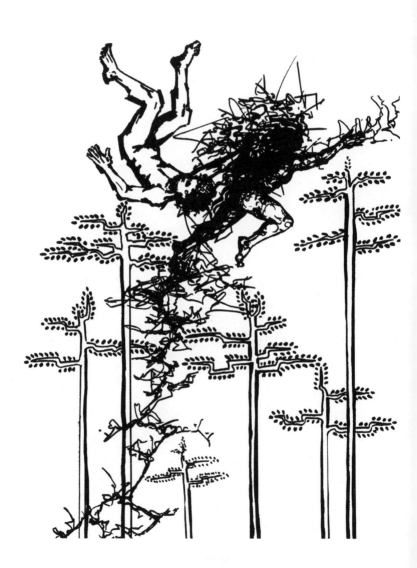

The Priest's Peculiar Wife

IN our parish a while ago there lived a young woman who fell in love with the curate at St. Botolph's, pursued him with mince pies and honey from her hives and watercolors she had made on her vacation in the Chablais. The young man was not hard to coax into similar feelings, and in a seemly season they were married. A few years later, the curate was presented to the living of St. Maude's in the next county, where he was installed as Vicar in his own right now, so we saw no more of him or of Fern, his wife.

Then, after a few years, we began to hear stories from those whose business took them over into that part of the world. It seems that our Fern had stopped presiding over the Ladies Guild, stopped attending the Parish Council meetings, and worst of all, had stopped entertaining at the Vicarage.

The vicar himself was seen to be plump and jolly and much as he had been, but his wife soon was hardly to be seen at all. Occasionally she'd be encountered walking quickly, in the gloaming of the evening or the day's first light, in some meadow or by the inconsequential stream they call a river in their vanity over there. In such encounters, the vicar's wife would acknowledge greetings and return them, eyes averted, and she would pass on without lingering to chat.

Soon the wits of the village began to pay close attention to the vicar's Sunday sermons and occasional feast day homilies. If he spoke of Hebrews and Philistines they were sure he was thinking of the baleful Delilah. If he spoke of Nazareth, they were certain he felt in his heart a grim contrast between the Holy Family and his own childless home and wildling wife.

For no child had come along to pin the girl down to her proper place. Speculation abounded. One officious person, a known troublemaker and frequenter of the public library, took it upon himself to write to the bishop, hinting and surmising and taking note with alarm. No answer came from the episcopal palace.

We in our town set to wondering. After all, she was one of ours, and her kin were all about us, each saner than the next, not a hint of night wandering. Should we do anything? A young man named Elphin (some parents just don't get the naming business) who had himself at one time been smitten with Fern decided to find out for himself. He was, I'm afraid, still keen on the girl.

Elphin saddled up and made his way to St. Maude's, and when he got there went boldly to the Vicarage. The aged housekeeper, a friendlier soul than most of her profession, received the young man courteously and installed him in the parlor. He waited.

After a bit the vicar came in, all smiles, and when he learned the object of Elphin's visit, explained that his lady wife was out on her charitable visits to the poor of the parish, but would surely be home within the quarter-hour, do wait. The vicar withdrew, and Elphin waited, comforting himself by communing with the cat asleep on the hearthrug.

Sure enough, in a few minutes Fern came rushing in, ruddy-cheeked, breathless, smiling to see him. She snatched his hand and dragged him to his feet.

"Come, we're going now. Why did it take you so long to come?"

Giving him no time to answer, she pulled him out the front door and down the path. At the road she unhitched his horse but instead of mounting it, slapped its haunch and sent it galloping away. Elphin watched aghast as his horse vanished towards the forest.

In that same direction Fern was tugging him now, "Come on, come on!" she kept urging. Soon she was running, and he had to run to keep up with her. Faster still, he did not know he could run so fast. Or that anyone could. In a few minutes they were moving so quickly he could barely feel the rocks and stubble they ran through. By now they had caught up his horse, and flashed past it.

Now they were in the trees, moved slower but still very fast. Time seemed to be running with them too, for Elphin was sure it was still afternoon when he came to the Vicarage — it seemed to be full night now, and when they stumbled at last into a grassy clearing and stopped, a great white moon shone down on them. They stood there, Elphin gasping for breath, Fern perfectly still. Elphin heard crashing in the brush around him, and in a minute his horse, all lathered with sweat, came limping to join them.

Fern searched along the ground, found what she was looking for and snatched it up: a handful of thick grass, and brought it to the horse's mouth. Quickly he swallowed it, shivered, and stood still, at peace.

Fern took Elphin by the shoulders, looked at him seriously, said: "I am a little cross with you, you've made me wait so long."

What could Elphin say? No one, to his knowledge, had ever waited for him.

"But I forgive you," she went on, "we still have all the time in the world."

At once she stripped off her clothes and stood naked before him. But it was not the body he had perhaps guiltily imagined. It was a strong body, rough skin, and her hair seemed to move by itself. And as she turned this way and that, he was shocked to see a great curving lissome tail, long and thick as a tiger's, sprouted from the base of her spine. But before he could process this and seek in folklore for a name, let alone an explanation, she had in some savage gesture torn his clothes away. And his body too was not the one he knew or remembered. For one thing, it felt no weariness now, and for another it was covered with a fine soft fur, deep fur, as if he were a mink or a fisher. But he wasn't dreaming, she had slapped him hard, and at the slap he felt pain and knowledge all at once. But what was it he understood? Sometimes we feel we understand, understand, but can't put words to what we know.

Before he could do much thinking, Fern whistled, and out of the woods came bounding a creature like an ape, its dense matted hair all blonde and bronze, and only through the happy grinning face could Elphin recognize the Vicar of St. Maude's. Elphin feared the vengeance of a jealous husband, but he need not have done so. In his deep parsonical voice the vicar intoned, "Welcome, brother, we have waited for thee."

And they were off! Running this way and that through the trees, and then back out on the road, the horse running with them, all at the same pace, and the horse had sack after sack on its back, and from these the vicar and his wife, and eventually, as he grew more confident or just more carefree, Elphin too would take handfuls of food and medicine and even money, and toss it at the doorways of houses and cottages and shops and inns. And all that while they saw no one, though there were lights in all the windows, and here and there someone singing, or playing Mendelssohn on the piano.

And so it went, every night week after week, until the first snow came to ____shire, and the nightly donations had to stop. One morning Elphin woke up in the little bedroom they had made his in the vicarage and found the house empty, the fire burned out. He dressed quickly, shivering, and looked around. On the dining room table a note: *Dear Elphin. Thank you. Forever, F.*

Outside, he found his own horse all saddled and looking well-fed. He climbed on and the horse by himself took off for our parish. And here Elphin still lives, sad and grateful, unwed still, still pining for Fern, whatever she was or is, hair greying now, happier dreaming than awake, doing what he can to feed the poor and make the children happy, all that business of love we call charity, the kind of love we feel when the one we love is far from us but the love is real. Ask Elphin. Elphin knows. For I am he.

Boxing Day 2016

The Cat and the Butterfly

ONCE upon a summer afternoon a child was sitting on the grass of her parents' house (though she thought of it as her grass) and looking at a butterfly, sulfur yellow, flipping and dipping and skipping around the flowers. So many kinds of flowers. And even flowers that are the same kind are so different from one another. She sighed. How can you know all the names? How can you tell them apart? They're as bad as people. Her Aunt Esther and her Uncle Thad are always together but they looked completely different. How can they be the same kind of thing? And she and her stupid brother Evan, no resemblance at all. How can she expect two irises to look alike? She liked that flower, so soft and at ease and quiet, and she loved the name, it had her own name for herself in it, I-, and that made it special.

While she was pondering these things, the butterfly, and sometimes more than one of him, kept adventuring in the flowers. And the girl wasn't the only spectator. The family cat (her cat, when she remembered to feed it) Gatto was watching the butterflies too, occasionally looking away from them to the little girl.

"Do you know what I'm doing?" the cat asked.

The girl wasn't too surprised. If her Aunt Miriam, the one with red hair and no uncle to go with her, could drink wine and dance on the table once, just once, anything could happen once. So why not the cat? It probably has a lot to say.

"No, Gatto, I don't know. What are you doing?"

"I'm flying the butterflies around to amuse you. You do like them, don't you?"

"Yes, I do, I really do. But don't they fly by themselves?" She thought that was the whole point of being a butterfly, to look like fresh butter and fly around.

"No," said the cat, "that is a common

mistake, no doubt produced by the silly English name — in German and French we don't make the mistake of thinking butterflies fly — Schmetterling! Papillon!"

"What are you talking about, cat?"

"Sorry, I was speaking a grade or two above your level. To put it simply: butterflies do not fly. They are flown. And we are the ones who fly them."

"You mean you and I we?"

"No, dear child, we cats. Cats stay indoors all winter long, hence no butterflies. But lots of flickering shadows from candles and Christmas trees and such. In winter we cats fly shadows around the house, to keep in practice."

"Why can't I fly butterflies if I want to?"

"Why indeed. No reason that I know. Not being myself a human, I have only a vague idea of what humans can or can't fly or otherwise control. If you can fly butterflies, you'd know it. Just try for a while — it takes (he said modestly) a certain amount of practice, a certain skill."

"Maybe I can do other things," she said a

little peevishly, "maybe things you can't do."

The cat was peaceable with that.

"Very likely you can. What have you tried?"

The girl thought a moment, then a moment more, looking furtively this way and that around the garden.

Then she spoke boldly.

"I can make a stone stand still!"

The cat seemed impressed.

"That is a very great gift, and of great use to us all. It makes our squadrons of butterflies look rather petty, if pretty. Think how horrible it would be if stones were moving around all the time, leaping through the air, skipping out from under you, and from under buildings and banks and cathedrals! Life would be awful if rocks could run around at will. Bless you, dear child. You have a great skill, and I would envy you if animals knew envy. But we just know the word, but can't feel what it means."

Then Gatto looked away, and went on flying butterflies around the irises.

Boxing Day 2016

The Girl in the Curtains

EVERY day on his way home from school Joseph would pass a building all by itself on a block with vacant lots all round it. The building was one common in the early 20th century, three floors of apartments above a ground floor with two stores, an entrance door between them giving access to the stairs. The store on the left sold shoes, the store on the right sold toys. Joseph was too old for most toys now, so he seldom looked in the windows.

All the more so because of what he could see from across the street — that was his natural path home anyhow, and he usually stayed on that sidewalk, walking past the garage and the coal merchant and the bookshop, but keeping a close eye on that building all by itself on the other side of the street.

Because of the curious fact that almost every single day as Joseph passed it at 3:10 on his way home from school, he would see in the window just above the T of Toyshop a girl behind the glass. No sooner did she notice him gazing up at her than she would whisk closed the curtain by which, half-concealed, she was always standing. She looked like a pretty girl.

This had been happening for years now, almost every school day, the glance, his fascinated gaze, the abrupt vanishing. Joseph wondered if she did that to every passerby or just to him. Joseph wondered too whether she stood there at the window all afternoon every day, or just on school days.

So he made it his business one Sunday afternoon, when everybody was sleeping off the enormous Sunday dinners of those days, to creep back, coming from the home direction not the school, and wearing a big overcoat of his Uncle Hans, with a cap pulled down over his eyes. Sure enough, the girl was there. This time, she was looking in his direction, and as soon as she saw him peering up at her from across the street, she fluffed the curtain out in front of her. But it did seem to Joseph that there had been a second or two of hesitation, as if the act of recognizing him in his disguise took conscious attention.

So it went on, from fifth grade to sixth to seventh, to eighth and finally now, eleventh grade, and Joseph a fine young adolescent getting ready for the world. And also getting ready to play the man, to address th world of women. This woman.

One Friday in November he could stand it no longer. As he shivered in the drizzle he looked up at her, and at once the cloth came between them. But this time he darted across the street and tried the entrance door. It opened at a touch. He hurried up the stairs before his resolution wavered, and pounded on the door of the apartment, first floor front, that must give entrance to the room where the girl stood.

The door swung open as if from the mere force of his knocking. Joseph stepped in, and heard the door close behind him. It was very bright in there.

As his eyes got used to the glare, he saw that the room, if it was a room, was very big. It stretched away into the distance, full of sun and sand. It looked like a desert, like a film he had seen once of the Arabian desert, just sand and yellows and shadows that seemed almost solid chunks of darkness, under a sky hot blue as a welding spark. At his feet he saw sand, clearly sand. There was no sign of the girl or her curtain or the window she stands at, stood at so many days, so many years. Just more desert, with a rise of mountain in the far distance. He was thirsty. He was afraid.

Behind him, where the door had been, a growling sound. He spun round and saw a fat little old man sitting cross-legged in sand, and making noises like a dog. Or a lion.

"You have come for my daughter at last," the man said.

"I came to see her, I have seen her for so many years, I wanted to know her, forgive me, I shouldn't have just come in like this. But I wanted to see her, really see her, and ask her why she always hides from me behind the curtain." Joseph surprised himself by saying so much, and so clearly, and by saying what he really meant.

"No," the old man said, "there is no curtain. I think it must be something in you, in your eyes. Maybe you have ..." He paused, as if seeking some technical term, for an ophthalmic condition, "...maybe you have shy eyes."

Joseph didn't know what to say. Maybe the man was right. But even so, where is the girl?

"Where is she, though, your daughter."

The old man laughed. "Oh you, you really do have shy eyes. She's right here, just look round you. She is the sunlight on the sand, the blue in the sky, the heat in the sand around your feet. She is everything you can see. Everything wants to show itself to you, yet people are afraid to see, their eyes are shy, or lazy, or afraid. For years you have not let yourself really see what you see. Now go to sleep a while. She'll come and tuck you in."

Joseph was overwhelmed with torpor and sank down into the nice soft warm sand. He felt someone's fragrant breath on his cheeks, on his mouth, and then he slept.

When he woke up, he was standing out in the street, facing his home. He walked mechanically in the right direction, thinking, or trying to think. He did not think he would ever see the girl again. But who knows?

Boxing Day 2016

Shadow Talk

"I WONDER what my shadow would say if it could talk," the boy wondered. He was sitting on the floor in the parlor, a nice thick Axminster carpet from Wanamaker's soft beneath him. And under it there was a special matting his mother had explained. It protects the rug and the floor and the feet and everything. Jute.

He was watching his shadow, half of it on the sideboard, half askew on the pale wall beside it. The part on the sideboard, right under the cut-glass bowl full of oranges, was the shadow of his left shoulder, the wall part his right shoulder. I am both places at once, he thought. A strong light was coming from behind him, the setting sun shining through the picture window.

But if the shadow could talk it would be another person, wouldn't it, so the part on

the sideboard would be the shadow's right arm, and the wall part his left. My right his left, just like a mirror, he thought. And sure enough, when he raised his left arm, the shadow raised its right arm.

This is confusing. A shadow is all black, no mouth, no eyes, and a reflection in a mirror has all the parts that I have. But somehow they're both me. But my left his right.

"Her right," the shadow said.

The boy wasn't sure but he thought he'd heard the shadow speak, a high mellow gentle voice, sounded like her right, or hurry out or something like that. Though the shadow has no mouth, so how can it speak? The boy decided to try an experiment.

"Hello, shadow," he called, loud. He reasoned that it might be an echo, after all, an echo is like the shadow of a sound.

"What do you want?" the shadow said.

This was clearly no echo.

"Are you really my shadow?"

"Whose else could I be — do you see anyone else in the room? We are alone. You are my Opacity, I am your shadow."

"What's an opacity?" Curiosity overcame his sense of strangeness in talking to the wall. Or the sideboard. Where was the mouth anyway?

"You are an Opacity, my special one. An Opacity is anything that blocks the light. By doing so, it forces the light to shape itself around the Opacity, leaving a more or less accurate image of the Opacity on any surface otherwise brightened by the light. This Image is a Shadow. I am one. You are my Opacity. You belong to me."

"But you're my shadow! So you belong to me."

"That also is true. We belong to you, but it's hard for you to control us. We're always changing, according to the light, the dark, the movements of our Opacities. For example, right now I have no legs because you're sitting on the floor with your knees drawn up to your chin, chatting with me. So I have no feet, no legs, no hands, no arms—your arms are wrapped round your knees. How inert I am, I'm like the shadow of a mountain, not a man. I mean a boy. But I have a head still, so I can talk to you."

"Why don't you sound like me, if you're my shadow?"

"Well, I'm much more learned than you, I've been around a lot, and you've made me mingle with the shadows of other people — your mother, your father, your friends at school — and when shadows mingle on a wall, when one shadow mingles with someone else's shadow, each shadow automatically knows everything the other shadows know. Shadows are of one substance, one flesh, all alike. It's automatic."

"That's scary, you know everything my father's shadow knows?"

"Yes, and your uncle's, and the priest who christened you, and the teacher who shook your hand when you graduated from kindergarten, and the mailman you talked to one day on the sidewalk, when he was all sweaty from the bright sun. All of them."

"But why doesn't your voice sound the least little bit like my voice?"

"Because a shadow is always the gender opposite her Opacity. I am what you would call a Girl Shadow, and will eventually be a

Woman Shadow as you get older — but there won't be any difference in me, only in you. I will follow your movements faithfully, and I'll try to understand why you do the things you do, silly things, stupid things, smart things. And when you grow up a little, you'll be able to ask me questions, and I will answer out of the great store of my knowing, and then you'll know some of what I know. You'll say Shadow, Shadow on the wall, how shall I make my true love call? And I will answer, Just stare at the wall and remember!"

"But I don't have a true love."

"That was just an example. You will have loves soon enough, true and otherwise. Be careful to ask me which is the true one. Meantime, always stare at the wall and remember."

The Leper's Touch

ONCE upon a time, hundreds and hundreds of years ago, there lived a leper. Like many lepers he came from a good family and had been a sturdy, affluent young man when the disease came upon him. The demons who cause leprosy, like many other Morbiferous Demons, do not want to waste their spores or seeds on the feeble or the fated. No, they prefer the plump to the meager, the young to the old. Leprosy demons want to live a long, relaxed life in their host, without much bothering to move from victim to victim.

So our leper had been robust as you please when the tell-tale bronze patches appeared, the white scurf, the odd failure of sensation here and there. His family was certainly supportive and capable of providing him with a secluded cottage to which his need-

ments would be brought by cautious though respectful servants.

Our leper, though, was of a melancholy bent (for Saturn is the lord of affliction and reflection both), and considered carefully what he ought to do. The conclusion to which he came was this: that he would embrace this terrible obstacle and take it somehow as a path. In his country at that time most lepers wandered around alone or in scruffy bands begging for provender. So he fitted himself out with warm clothes and set out on his life of exile. His weeping parents presented him with a little silver bell to ring, to warn strangers of his condition as he approached them, as the law required. He turned and smiling through his own tears rang the little bell at them and set off.

You can imagine his life for the next few years, wandering, being shunned, being helped, being fed, going hungry, freezing, sweltering. We still live in the same world, nothing has changed, you know as well as I do what it felt like to go day after day in all seasons on this planet. Where to sleep.

Where to bathe. Where to void. Enough said.

Five long years our leper wandered through his country, occasionally drifting across the borders of other princedoms, never going far, though, from those whose language was his own.

One pleasant spring day, really the first warm day of the year, he stopped and carefully wiped the sweat from the sores on his face, then bent to drink from a clear stream, just a rill, running alongside the road. As he drew near the water, he was shocked to see how ugly and deformed he had become. It felt very strange to gulp the water then, as if he were drinking ugliness, accepting, his own ruination. I accept what I am given, he thought, may all be well.

Later that day he came into a town, always ringing his silver bell (the envy of all the lepers, and a few little children too young to know anything but the bright silver, the sound). People drew away from him, naturally. But there, on the ground, a man lay groaning. At first the leper thought the man was drunk already and not even midday yet. But then he heard him cry for help and groan, and cry again. As his eyes caught sight of the leper, he called, please, you, please, help me.

It had been a long time since anyone had asked the leper for anything — a leper's life is all receiving, it seems — so he was a little unsure of what to do. He rang his bell loud as he could and approached the man.

"Give me a hand," the man called, "I am sick, I can't get up."

Obediently the leper held out his healthier hand, the man took hold, the leper pulled with all his little strength and the man was able to rise.

"Thank you, sir. I feel much better now, much better indeed."

The color had come back into the man's face, and he looked ten years younger than he had a moment before. He smiled at the leper and walked away.

An old woman had been watching from a doorway, and now, clutching her chest, she boldly came towards the leper. He rang his bell and backed away, but she moved quickly.

"Touch me," she cried, "touch me here,"

she said, pointing her thumb at her chest. Timidly, the leper lifted his hand to her chest.

"The pain is gone!" she cried, grabbed the leper's hand, kissed it and hurried away, and was soon surrounded by people asking and judging. The leper was edging away, uneasy about the whole business, not knowing what to think. And a voice inside him seemed to say You don't need to think. Just carry on.

The leper paused by the church steps and a young mother came towards him, leading a pretty young child limping painfully, his left leg half-genuflecting at each step.

"Please!" the mother said.

The leper bent and touched the boy's leg, the boy gasped, crumpled to the ground, immediately jumped up and walked around, danced around laughing, no trace of a limp.

That morning the leper must have cured or eased the pain of twenty-seven people in the town. By evening he was sitting alone on the church steps, a few people watching him warily, reverently, fearfully, from across the little square.

At the ringing of the angelus, the air darkening already, the leper got up and made his way out of town. When he bent to drink from the next stream he met (for lepers as you know are not allowed to drink from wells or fountains), he could hardly see his face in the swift water, but what he saw scared him a little — he looked much older, and the marks of his condition, the swollen cheeks of the lion mask (as they called it), much puffier, gashed. And his hands felt strange.

And so it went on for the next year or so, the leper becoming the healer of all, and every healing weakening him further. I accept what I am given and I give what I can, is how he thought about it. Obscurely he knew that the demons of his disease were not happy about him curing so many people — and even a sick horse once, and a moaning cow — so they were punishing him; yet didn't they realize they were ruining their own residence by doing so? Ah, sickness is a mystery, he thought, as big a mystery as birth and death.

By now his hands were like claws, he could barely hold his bell, and there was not much left of his nose. He thought maybe he should make his way to his home, maybe his family needed healing too. Why hadn't he thought of that before.

He set out homeward but never got there. He met so many crippled people and ailing folk along the way, he had to heal them all, had to touch each one, and at every touch there was less and less of him until one day when he bent down to drink he did not rise again.

The bishop of those parts consecrated a small plot of ground adjacent to the real churchyard, and men wearing handkerchiefs over their noses and mouths, handkerchiefs soaked in lavender and thyme, carried the dead leper to the place and buried him there, with much Latin spoken.

For a time, people would come to the grave hoping to be healed, and some of them were. There was even talk of declaring him a saint, but no one could remember his ever having practiced religion. And furthermore, nobody knew his name. You can't have a saint without a name.

Childermas 2016

The Rainbow

ONCE upon a time three girls were whiling away the summer afternoon in the barnyard, talking about their boyfriends real or proposed. A sudden squall came up over the prairie from the west with drenching rain. The girls hurried for shelter into the barn, careful not to smoke near the hay. The rain lasted only a few minutes, the storm cloud passed, and the girls came out into the sweet air the rain had freshened.

To their delight, they saw a big, very clear rainbow above them, with its great arch seeming to come to earth very nearby, just over the woodlot, or maybe even into the trees.

One girl started singing the rainbow song from The Wizard of Oz, and the other two giggled appreciatively. But she soon ran out

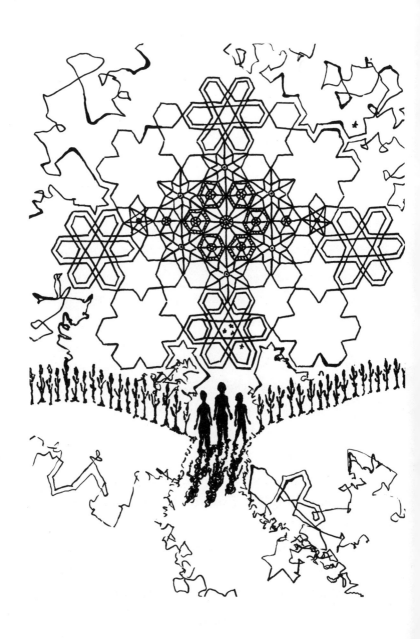

of words, so they just watched the rainbow.

"I wonder if there really is a pot of gold at the end of the rainbow," one said, idly.

"But which end?" said the skeptic of the group, a girl on her third steady boyfriend, which gave her opinions weight. "Imagine traveling for years and getting there and finding out it was at the other end."

That left them glum for a few moments, and their thoughts were turning to other matters when the third girl said "But how close it looks! It seems to be coming down almost right here. Let's go and look!"

So off they went, carrying no provisions — how far could it be? They climbed the rail fence (straightest line to the nearby rainbow) and made their way across the cornfield. An onlooker would have seen three heads from time to time, or two, or just the head of the tallest girl, bouncing along, and would note the swooshing as if of small winds through the tall standing corn.

Once across the half-mile of field, they entered the small woodlot, expecting at any moment to see the darkness in among the trees light up with all the colors of the spectrum. And so they did, but not until they had walked deep into the woods, and one of the girls was already beginning to think of turning back, and another had actually whined a quiet how-long-are-we-supposed-to-go-on.

Then they were there. They stumbled into a clearing and there it was, the graceful arc blazing down its colors onto the brown earth. The girls were amazed, but felt no fear, somehow, and also felt no heat, for all the brightness before them.

And there were three young men in front of the rainbow, they seemed almost to be part of it, and the strange thing is that although they didn't seem to be wearing any clothes, they weren't naked either.

One young man, whose hair was yellow as corn and his skin ruddy, spoke first.

"Welcome, ladies of the prairie. We have come for you."

The second youth, curiously pale, almost greenish, lay on the ground and waved cheerfully. The third young man was very dark, almost blue-black hair like a hero in a cartoon, and such dark skin! He too was smiling at the girls.

It was he who spoke next, very formally.

"It has come to our attention that women who reside on the prairie — itself part of the great circumglobal savannah or grassland, like those of Mongolia, the steppe of Central Asia, the puszta of Hungary — have more need of color than those who dwell in cities or jungles. Are we correct in so assuming?"

The girls didn't know what to say. One of them was thrilled to hear the word 'dwell' used in an actual spoken sentence, not in poetry. Another girl said, "I guess so…"

"So here we are," said Green from the ground, "which colors will be yours? I'm the simplest, but I cover the most ground. Roy here (pointing to the blond fellow who had first spoken) is fiery, hard to handle, but said to be a lot of fun. My blue bro Biv, he's moody, contemplative, a real philosopher, and no harm in him. Take your pick."

Now it so happened that each set of characteristics described appealed perfectly to the moods and wishes of one particular girl, so each girl knew at once her proper... proper what?

"What are you going to be to us," the skeptic asked, her eyes on Biv, "husbands, lovers, friends, teachers, children...?"

"Wait and see," answered Roy.

So with an inwardly breathed prayer of Whatever, the girls went to their chosen ones, and at the first embrace each girl fell asleep, and lay on the soft earth while the afternoon hummed away and the night came to know the prairie.

They woke when it was very dark, dark of the moon too, but the stars were clear enough, though the trees hid most of them. The girls woke all at the same time. No rainbow. They reached out and found each other, got up. They knew enough not to say anything. Curiously, they didn't miss the rainbow, or the young men. They felt oddly refreshed.

It didn't take them long to find their way home. The stars over the cornfield were magnificent, they'd never seemed so bright before, and in the twinkle of each the girls could see (but none of the three mentioned it) gleams and flickers of colors in the crystal white of their shine.

"We are very lucky ladies," one of the girls said.

"We know what we know," said the skeptic.

"We know who we are," said the third.

And when they got home each went to her bed, but all three of them went on dreaming this same dream that you and I are dreaming now. What color are you?

Childermas 2016

In addition to many books in various genres, mostly poetry, **ROBERT KELLY** has published five collections of short fiction with McPherson & Company: *A Transparent Tree*, *Doctor of Silence*, *Cat Scratch Fever*, *Queen of Terrors*, and *The Logic of the World*. He teaches in the Written Arts Program at Bard College. His two most recent books are long poems, *Calls* and *The Caprices*.

EMMA O'DONNELL POLYAKOV studied art at Bard College, and currently teaches and writes about religion. She is Assistant Professor of Religious and Theological Studies at Merrimack College, and the author of *Remembering the Future: The Experience of Time in Jewish and Christian Liturgy*.